12/2018

KAREN HESSE

The Music of Dolphins

SCHOLASTIC INC.

New York Toronto London Auckland
Sydney Mexico City New Delhi Hong Kong

ACKNOWLEDGEMENTS

I wish to extend sincere thanks to the following good humans for their insight and counsel: Heather Ahrenholz, Eileen Christelow, Jill Daniel, Esther Evenson, David Hall, Melissa Harman of the Clearwater Marine Science Center, The Immigration and Naturalization Service, Gayle Jamison, Liza Ketchum, Fran and Jerry Levin, Louise McDevitt, Robert and Tink MacLean, Ana Lyla and Esther Mosak, Maryann Ogden, Sunset Sam, Arlyn Sharpe, Kevin Weiler, and the flight crews at the United States Coast Guard Clearwater Station, particularly LJG Lisa Blow and Lieutenant Tom Gauntt. Also to be acknowledged are my daughters, Kate and Rachel, for whom I am forever thankful not only for their insight and counsel, but for their steadfast belief and their joyful companionship. And finally I wish to acknowledge Brenda Bowen, who never fails to hear the beauty in my rough music.

ISBN 978-0-590-89798-3

Text copyright © 1996 by Karen Hesse
Cover images © 2005 by Darren Hopes
All rights reserved. Published by Scholastic Inc.
SCHOLASTIC and associated logos are trademarks
and/or registered trademarks of Scholastic Inc.

44 43 42 41 40   18 19 20

Printed in the U.S.A.   40

Book design by Elizabeth B. Parisi

To Randy.
For twenty-five years you have kept me afloat.

The Music of Dolphins

I swim out to them on the murmuring sea. As I reach them, their circle opens to let me in, then re-forms. The dolphins rise and blow, floating, one eye open, the other shut in half sleep.

Joyful with the coming day, I splash and whistle at a milky sun. The dolphins wake and whistle too. They are suddenly and fully aware. The ocean fills with their sound. Flukes slapping. Quick calls rising and falling. We slide under and over each other, racing through the morning waves, riding the misty lid of the sea.

Three gulls sit on the soft shoulder of a swell. So quiet, I come with my dolphin cousins, up from below, and scare the bobbing birds. The gulls rise, screaming mad. We laugh and laugh, bright beads of dolphin noise, while above the birds dip and cry.

A cool wind tickles the swells and one free gull feather floats on the face of the sea. My dolphin cousin grabs it and darts below. Under she goes, then up again, faster, springing into the air. She passes the feather to the next cousin who takes her turn diving, running, playing with it. Their game spins me in the waves. The small hairs rise on my arms.

While we play, the old ones search for something to eat. They flash their blinding sound into a school of silver fish. As my dolphin family swims, mouths open, through the thick school, I climb out of the sea.

Standing on the small beach, the mangrove swamp at my back, I hear a sound over the rush and hiss of the tide, over the whistles and squeaks of my dolphin family feeding, over the splashing and tail slapping. I hear a sound pushing at the air. It beats like a giant heart. Airplane. I see it far-off, pressed against the roof of the sky. It growls a distant warning.

I turn away to feed on molting crab, juicy roots, ribbons of salt weeds.

The plane comes closer. The sound of it shakes my bones. My skin shivers, like an orca is coming.

My dolphin mother senses danger, my smooth, beautiful mother with her wise eyes and her spotted flukes. I hear her; she calls me back to sea. I want to go to her. I am afraid of the plane. But I must find water to drink first and give my mother more time to eat. She does not eat enough because of me.

I make my way through the wet and tangled roots of the mangrove, creeping toward the opposite side of the cay. I reach the long rocks where rain gathers in wide, deep pools. There is much water today. I cup my hands and drink. The water is cool with a hint of salt. When my hands can gather no more, I scoop the water into a shell, and when the shell brings nothing, I suck at what remains with my lips.

While I drink, the plane flies close again. No longer is it a distant gleaming. It comes too near. It is not like other planes, more like an ugly fish with spinning fins on its back.

Something drops from it. I try to hide. The wind from the plane makes my long hair fly. The mangrove pitches and roars. I am pounded by spinning air. The earth shakes and circles of sand rise around me. I sense the frantic whistle of my mother, but the sound is lost in the scream of the plane.

And then a man jumps out. He comes after me. I slip deeper into the mangroves. But the man is too big, too fast.

I cannot get away.

WILD CHILD FOUND ON ISLAND OFF CUBA

MIAMI, FL, Dec. 5 — "I thought she was a mermaid at first," said Lieutenant Junior Grade Monica Stone. "Her hair hung down to her feet and she was covered with seaweed." On closer examination the flight crew on the Coast Guard Jay Hawk realized they'd spotted not a mermaid but a human child.

Their mission started as a routine surveillance flight over the Cay Sal bank in the waters between Florida and Cuba. The crew, composed of Stone, pilot Nicholas Fisk, and flight mechanic Gary Barnett, had flown hundreds of search-and-rescue missions over this section of water. But this mission was unlike any they'd flown before.

After the initial observation of the child, the crew radioed Miami and awaited clearance to land. Hovering above, they videotaped the girl. "Gary threw the pump can out to her on a parachute. Pump cans hold food, blankets, first aid. Most people run toward them. This girl ran away, hiding in the mangroves. She had this really weird way of moving, like the ground

was rolling under her feet. Gary climbed down and walked toward her, holding out his hand."

"She was so strange," said Barnett. "The way she acted. More like an animal than a human."

Once they got her aboard the helicopter, Stone wrapped the naked girl in a blanket. "She was making a high-pitched cry, like a seagull," said Stone. "Her respiration was odd, popping out of her, like breathing was something she had to remember to do."

Stone, a communications and public relations specialist, speaks fluent English, Spanish, and French. The child either couldn't or wouldn't respond to efforts to communicate in any language.

Her height and body development suggest a girl somewhere between the ages of eleven and sixteen years, said Stone. Her weight, in the vicinity of one hundred pounds, is at least ten percent hair.

"Most refugees we pick up look as if they've been at sea a couple of days. Their eyes are bloodshot. They're dehydrated," said Barnett. "But they still look human. This girl was streaked with salt. There were barnacles growing on her, for crying out loud. The condition of her skin — she had circular scars all over her face and body — she

4

had to be living in the sea a long time."

"Mila [the name given her by the Coast Guard crew] is definitely human, but there's something about her, something wild," Stone said.

The Immigration and Naturalization Service; the Bahamian, Haitian, and Cuban governments; and a team of medical specialists working under grants issued by the National Institute of Mental Health are disputing custody of the newly discovered wild child, the second such discovery in as many months.

True wild children are a rare occurrence, said Dr. Elizabeth Beck, research professor of cognitive and neural systems at Boston University. "Feral children are an invaluable resource for studying the role language and socialization play in the making of a human being."

Beck has designed a unique facility at the Charles River campus to stimulate a "human" response in these children. She attributes the public's interest in them to the fact that wild children like Shay, the fragile girl discovered in Idaho's Salmon River Mountains, and Mila have much to teach us about ourselves.

On the short flight back from Anguila Cays to the mainland, the distraught girl kept thumping her cheek against the window of the Jay Hawk and squealing. Barnett used his hand as a cushion between the girl's head and the hard surface of the helicopter wall. Her squeal could be heard over the engine chop, like an animal crying.

"It was like she was calling to someone down there," Stone said.

Stone poured water into a cup and offered it to the girl.

"She touched the water with the tip of her finger, then touched her finger to her tongue," said Stone. "Slowly she extended her palms toward me, cupped, sealed tight. I poured water into her waiting hands and she drank from them."

"There was just something about her," said Stone. "From the moment I laid eyes on her I wanted to do things for her, give her things. She was visibly exhausted by the time we landed in Miami, but by then at least she understood we meant her no harm. Right before we delivered her to I.N.S. she leaned forward and studied me with one eye, then slowly turning, she studied me with the other. It still amazes me every time I think about it — the way she connected with us. I've never felt anything like it."

One

Doctor Beck says, Where is the ear?

I show a picture of the ear.

Doctor Beck says, Good, Mila. Where is the eye?

I show a picture of the eye.

Doctor Beck says, Good, Mila. Where is the nose?

I show a picture of the hair.

Doctor Beck says, No, Mila.

The nose is not in the hair. The nose is here. In front of the face. Doctor Beck shows a picture of the nose.
Doctor Beck says, Where is the nose, Mila?

I show a picture of the nose.

Doctor Beck says, Good. Good, Mila.

I like good.

Two

The helper is Sandy. Sandy says,
I have a present for you, Mila.
Sandy says, This present is
to eat. This present is good fish.
Do you want to eat this good
fish, Mila?

I say, No.
The fish is not good. The fish is
dead.

Sandy is not happy. I like Sandy
happy.

Three

Doctor Beck says, What is this?
Doctor Beck shows a picture.
The picture talks. It says, Girl.
Doctor Beck says, What is this,
Mila?

I say, Girl.

Doctor Beck says, Good. Good,
Mila. What is this?
Doctor Beck shows a picture.
The picture talks. It says, Boy.
Doctor Beck says, What is this,
Mila?

I say, Boy.

Doctor Beck shows a picture.
The picture talks. It says,
Dolphin.
Doctor Beck says, What is this,
Mila?

I say, Dolphin. Dolphin! Good
good dolphin!
I like to see the picture of
dolphin.

Doctor Beck says, Very good,
Mila. Tell me. What are you?
A girl or a dolphin?

I show a picture. The picture
talks. It says, Dolphin.

I say, Dolphin.

Doctor Beck says, No, Mila.

Doctor Beck shows a mirror.

Doctor Beck is in the mirror. A girl is in the mirror.
Doctor Beck says, Okay, Mila. Tell me, what are you? A girl or a dolphin?

I look in the mirror. I look at the picture. The picture talks. It says, Girl.
I say, Girl.

Doctor Beck says, Yes. Girl. Good, Mila. You are a girl.

Four

Sandy is here. Sandy says, Look, Mila. I have a book. It is a fish book.

I come to Sandy.

Sandy says, Show me the tail of the fish, Mila.

I am showing the fish tail.

Sandy says, Good, Mila. Show me the big rocks.

I am showing the big rocks.

Sandy says, Good, Mila. Show me the sea?

I say, Sandy come.

Sandy says, No, Mila. Show me the sea in the book.

I want to show Sandy the good sea.

Sandy wants the picture in the book.

I show the picture in the book. I make Sandy happy.

Five

I am going to see another girl.

The girl is little.
The girl is different, not like
Doctor Beck and the others.
The girl is different like me.

I say my dolphin name to the
girl.

The girl looks at me.

I say my dolphin name again.

The girl makes a laugh.

Doctor Beck and Sandy and the others like the laugh.

Doctor Beck says to the girl, Shay. This is Mila.
Doctor Beck says, Mila. This is Shay.

I say the word *Shay*.

Sandy writes in a book, *Mila says Shay*.

Doctor Beck says, Shay is like you, Mila. Shay is learning to talk. You and Shay can work together. Who can show me a thing we wear?

I show a picture of boots. I say, boots. I have boots. Doctor Beck says boots are for rain only. My ears like to hear boots all the time. I make my good boots to talk like the dolphin.

Doctor Beck says, Good, Mila.

Shay is not showing. Shay is not saying.

Doctor Beck says, Who can tell me what you do with a fork?

I show a picture of eating.
I say, Eat.

Doctor Beck says, Good, Mila.

Shay is not showing. Shay is not saying.

Doctor Beck says, Who can tell me what you do when you are cold?

I am watching Shay.

I am walking to Shay.

I am showing Shay a gentle hand.

Shay is a soft hair girl. Shay is a big eyes girl. Shay is a little little girl.

I am looking in the face of Shay.

Shay is not showing. Shay is not saying.

But I am hearing Shay with no words.

Six

In the night, Doctor Beck
comes into my room.
Doctor Beck sees Sandy is
sleeping in the chair.
Doctor Beck says to Sandy, Go
home. You need to sleep.

I say, Sandy wants to stay.

Doctor Beck says, No, Mila.
Sandy wants to go home. We all
need to go home sometimes.

I say, I am not going home.

Sandy is watching me.

Doctor Beck is watching me. Doctor Beck says, Soon you will go home, Mila. Soon we will all move to a home together where we will eat and sleep and play.

I am happy. I am touching the hand of Doctor Beck. I say, We go home to the sea.

Doctor Beck says, No. Not to the sea.

I am not understanding.

Doctor Beck says, We go to a house.

I say, A house in the sea.

Doctor Beck says, No. Not in the sea, Mila. A house here, in Boston.

I come to Sandy.

Sandy makes gentle hands on me.

I want to go with Sandy and Doctor Beck. But I want to go to the sea.

Sandy says, Let me stay with Mila tonight, Doctor Beck.

Doctor Beck says, Yes. Okay. If you want. Stay.

I say, Another time we go to the sea, Doctor Beck. Yes?

Doctor Beck is a tired face.

Doctor Beck is a tired voice. Doctor Beck says, Another time, Mila.

Seven

So good.
I have Sandy when going to sleep. I have Sandy when waking up. I have Sandy to play all the time. Now I am not only.

Doctor Beck comes. Doctor Beck tells Sandy to give me a swimsuit.

Sandy says, Mila, you will like this.

Sandy says, Here are pictures of a girl getting ready to swim.

Here she is in her swimsuit. Do
you want to swim like the girl?

I say, Yes!
I put on the swimsuit. The
swimsuit is funny little skin
clothes.
I put on my good boots.
I am ready.
I say, Shay can swim too.

We go to Shay and Doctor
Troy.
I show Shay the picture of the
girl getting ready to swim.
I say, Come, Shay.

Shay is happy. Shay is holding
my hand. Shay is coming to
swim with me.

Outside is good warm sun. No more cold.
Outside is many things to see.
Outside is good for to breathe.
Good for to walk. Good for so many things to hear.

Doctor Beck shows me to go inside a very big house.

There is water in the house! I am hearing water! I say, Come fast, Shay!

Shay cannot come fast. Only hop, hop, hop.

I find the water myself. It is a bad smell. It is a bad taste. But it is water!

I am jumping into the water

with my clothes. I make dolphin talk. Squeak and whistle. I am laughing and splashing.

Sound is everywhere. Inside me, outside me. Good water sound in the big room.

I am moving fast and fast in the water. It makes my eyes to hurt but I am so happy to swim. I say, Come, Shay. Come in the water.

Shay is putting hands over her ears.

But Sandy comes in the water.

I am going around and around. So quiet, I come behind Sandy. I make a big splash and Sandy drinks the water and coughs.

I am laughing. The sound is going everywhere in the big room. I am hearing with good water ears every little sound.

A boy is coming into the room. He is tall like Doctor Beck.

Doctor Beck says, Hello, Justin. Doctor Beck is not looking at me. She is looking at the boy Justin. She is not touching the boy but she is with the boy. The boy is made very pretty. Good arms and legs. Hair is wet sand, like Doctor Beck.

I come to the side and splash Doctor Beck and the boy. The boy snaps at me like the angry dolphin. The boy snaps at Doctor Beck.

I laugh and laugh and swim away.

The boy goes.

I am splashing water on Sandy. I am so happy.
I say, Doctor Beck, I can stay here and sleep here in the water room with Sandy all the time?

Doctor Beck says, No. This is not a place to sleep, Mila. Only to swim. It is time to go back to the hospital. Come out of the water.

I do not want to go.

Doctor Beck says, You can come here again, Mila. I promise.

A promise is like a mother dolphin going away, then coming back with sweet fish for her baby. A promise is a good thing.

Eight

Sandy shows a picture of the water room. She says, The place we went yesterday is called a pool. Sandy says, Tell me what a pool is, Mila.

Doctor Beck and Sandy think I am a stupid fish.

Sandy says, No one thinks you are a stupid fish. This is how humans learn. By using the words again and again.

I say, A pool is a bad taste, bad eyes, bad nose place to swim.

Sandy says, Good, Mila.
Sandy says, Tell me what is the sea.

I say, The sea is a big home where all the time is swimming and all the time is singing and all the time is touching in the big wet.

Outside my room is standing Doctor Beck and the boy Justin. Justin says words to Doctor Beck. Justin has anger in his voice. Doctor Beck has anger too. But I am hearing another sound in Justin and Doctor Beck, something not anger.

In my room Doctor Beck brings a machine.
Doctor Beck says, This is a tape recorder.

Doctor Beck touches a button and I hear whales.

Whales!

Whales! Whales! Whales! I am so happy to hear whales.

My room is very small. I say, Doctor Beck, where are the whales?

Sandy says, There are not any whales, Mila. Only their sound. The whale sound is in the tape machine.

Whale sound is everywhere in my room. I am singing with the whales! I am talking with the whales.

Sandy and Doctor Beck see me sing

the whale song. Talk the whale talk.

I am so happy.

Justin is looking through the window into the room at me.

I say, Come in and listen to the whales.

Justin shakes his head, no. He walks away.

Nine

Sandy says, My father is sick.

This picture father, this word *father*, makes me think of big arms and a good smile.

Sandy says, I will be away for a little time, Mila. I must go to my family.

I say, What is family?

Sandy says, Family is people you love and care for, people who love and care for you.

I am thinking.
I say, We are family.

Sandy says, Yes. We are family. But I have another family. My other family has a sick father.

I say, Does Doctor Beck have another family?

Sandy says, Yes. Doctor Beck has her son, Justin. Justin is another family to Doctor Beck.

I say, Does Shay have another family?

Doctor Beck says, Yes. But her family cannot see her anymore.

I say, Why can the family of Shay not see her? Is there a problem with the eyes?

Doctor Beck says, No. Not their eyes. They cannot see Shay because they do not know a good way to love and care for her.

I have another family too. Dolphin family. The ones who love and care for me. The ones I love and care for. Can they see me again?
I say, Sandy, can the dolphins see me again?

Sandy is looking at Doctor Beck.

Doctor Beck says, Perhaps. Perhaps they can see you again, Mila.

Ten

Doctor Beck says, Come, Mila. While Sandy is away, you can be the teacher. Tell me which fish to point to.

I say, I am not listening, Doctor Beck.

Doctor Beck says, Of course you are listening, Mila.

I say, If Sandy is going, I am alone. In the day and in the night, I am alone.

Doctor Beck says, Sandy has gone to her father. She will come back.

I say, You can stay with me until Sandy comes back.

Doctor Beck says, No, Mila. I must go home each night to Justin.

I think of Doctor Beck and Justin. Like dolphin mother and dolphin baby. I am understanding.

I say, Did Sandy take the whale song to her father?

Doctor Beck says, No. I took the whale song, Mila.

I am looking at the hands of Doctor

Beck. I am looking in the pockets of Doctor Beck. I say, Where is the whale song? I can hear the whale song?

Doctor Beck says, No. When you hear the whale song, you don't pay attention to your work.

I say, If I am doing good work, can the whale song come back?

Doctor Beck says, Yes. The whale song can come back.

I say, If I am doing good work, can Sandy come back?

Doctor Beck says, Yes. Sandy will come back.

I say, When? When does Sandy come back?

Doctor Beck says, Soon.

I say, When is soon?

Doctor Beck makes her hand over her hair.
Doctor Beck says, Come, Mila. Do you want to visit Shay?

I say, Yes!
I am happy to visit Shay.

In the room of Shay, Doctor Troy is frowning.

Shay is sitting on the floor. She is rocking and rocking. Shay is not listening to Doctor Troy.

Shay sees me. She hops to me.

I touch the soft hair of Shay. I make a gentle hand on the little face of Shay. It is good, so good, to be with Shay.

In the quiet night, I go to the room of Shay. I make a warm nest on the floor by her bed. I can sleep in the room with Shay with one ear open to listen and one eye open to watch.

Eleven

Doctor Beck is giving work to Shay and to me.

Doctor Beck says, If you are waiting seven days for Sandy to come back and five days are finished, how many more days do you have left to wait? Doctor Beck shows with her fingers.

I say, Two.
I like to play these games.

Doctor Beck says, Good. Very good, Mila.

Doctor Beck says, Who can find the swimmer?

I can make the computer show a swimmer, easy.

Doctor Beck says, Good, Mila. Can you help Shay find the swimmer?

Shay looks all the time to me. She is all the time touching me. I am happy, so happy for the touch of Shay.

Justin comes. He watches me play the computer. He tells Doctor Beck to get me a better game.

Doctor Beck and Justin make the laugh.

I come over and make the laugh too, but Justin goes away.

Twelve

Doctor Beck says, Today is an important day. Today we move to our new house. You will like the house, Mila. All the doctors will live there with you. We will eat and sleep all in the same house. No more doctors going away at the end of the day.

I say, Is Sandy coming?

Doctor Beck says, Yes, of course. Sandy is coming. She is waiting for us at the house right now.

We go in a car to the new house.

The sun is hot and good. I am happy to be outside. But I have a worry.

I say, Doctor Beck, how can Sandy find the new house? There are many houses. How can Sandy know the house where we are going?

Doctor Beck says, Don't worry, Mila. I told you. Sandy is there.

Listen. Let me tell you about the house. You have your own bedroom! Your window looks out over the Charles River. Justin thought you would like that. I will come and get you every morning. We will all eat breakfast together in the big dining room. The house has a classroom for you and Shay to work together all the time. Look, you can see the back of the house from here. That's your window, right up there.

I am not listening. I see water.

Water! It is not big like the ocean, but it is not little like the pool.
I am out of the car running to the water.
I go over the road and into the water, swimming and swimming in my clothes, going with the good tide. I dive in the water. The water is not good to see in. It is all clouds. But it is much water.

I call my dolphin name. I call again and wait. First there is no answer. Then I hear.

But what I hear is not dolphin. What I hear is human.

Sandy! Sandy is calling me.

I swim to the shore fast. I am happy, happy to see Sandy.

Sandy is smiling for me. But I feel another thing in Sandy.

I say, I am so good to see you. Why are you sad?

Sandy makes a gentle hand on my face.
Sandy says, My father died, Mila.

I understand to die. I understand from the dolphin days.

Sandy and Doctor Beck take me to the new house.

The new house is good brown sand outside. Inside, the house has a room with a very big table. The house has a room with many soft chairs. The house has a big room with computers and many games. The house has a room with good little caves filled with food smells.

I see a room for Shay to sleep and Doctor Beck and Sandy and Doctor Troy.

Doctor Beck says, This room is for my son, Justin. And this room, Mila, is for you.

The room has a little window in the door. Shay has a little window in her door. No one else has windows in their doors.

Doctor Beck says, Welcome home, Mila.

Thirteen

A man comes. He is from the government.

Doctor Beck says the government is made of men and women who listen and talk about ideas and give money.

This man gives the money for us to live in the house. The man from the government watches me play with Doctor Beck. He watches me play with Sandy. He reads what I write on the special computer. He says, Can she operate this thing without help?

Doctor Beck says, Yes. She can.

The man of the government is watching me. He says, Mila is making good progress.

Making progress is when I talk words. Making progress is when I write on the computer. Making progress is when I wear clothes. Making progress is when I sleep in a bed and eat the dead fish.

Shay wears clothes. She sleeps in a bed and eats the dead fish. But Shay does not like the computer. Shay says only little words. One word. Then one word. Shay talks in a little voice not easy to hear.

Doctor Beck asks me to try the computer without help.

I can do it!

Fourteen

My name is Mila. Mila is the name the others give me. The ones who found me. Mila is miracle.

Miracle is when something is very, very difficult, but it happens.

Sandy says if I live in the sea for thirteen years, I am a miracle.

I am Mila.

Sandy gives a miracle to me today. The miracle is music.

Music is many things to hear, like in the sea. The music is made by a man named Winter.

I listen to the music. It is little sounds and little sounds together to make something so big. It is a bird singing and a whale singing and a people singing. It is so many sounds I cannot name. To hear it, it makes a little crying in my eyes.

I love the music.
I listen and listen. My legs and arms swim in the music.
My dolphin boots squeak in the music.

Doctor Beck says, You are dancing, Mila.

Dancing is very good. My inside hums, like with dolphin questions.

I say, Can we give music to Shay?

Doctor Troy brings Shay to the classroom.

I say, Listen, Shay. I make the music begin.

Shay is looking in my eyes. I am moving Shay

in a circle. But Shay is not hearing the music. Shay is not feeling the music. The music is in her ears, it is in her bones, but Shay cannot feel it.

How can Shay not feel the music?

Fifteen

Doctor Beck says, Mila, you need sleep.
She says, You listen to music all the night when
you should sleep. The others in the house hear
the music also. We need sleep.

I know Justin hears the music. Sometimes he
comes in and sits in the corner of my room and
listens with me. His hair is in his face and his
skin is creased like the new dolphin just born
and his chin falls down, but the music is inside
him.

Doctor Beck says if I do not stop playing the
music all night, she must take the music to another place where I cannot have it.

I remember she took the whale song from me.
I hold the tape in my hands.

My music, I tell Doctor Beck. My music.

In the tired eyes of Doctor Beck I see something danger.

Sandy says, Mila is learning.

Doctor Beck makes a hard face.

Sandy says, We can give Mila something to hear the music in her ears only.

Doctor Beck says, Perhaps. But she still needs to sleep.

I go to the window. Sandy comes to the window with me. Outside the trees have new colors and the wind blows a leaf up and up over the water.

Sandy asks, Does it make you sad to see the river, Mila?

I remember a warm sea. With many dolphins. I have a hunger to eat the good fish, to swim with the fast dolphins. I cannot forget my dolphin mother. The good strong touch of her. I cannot forget my dolphin cousins.

But I love this life too. I love the life with so many things to do with hands and eyes and nose and mouth and ears. We make food in the big kitchen. We wash the dishes. We go to the store and the bank. We write words and draw pictures. We walk and ride and swim and play.

Doctor Beck says, Do you remember a time before the dolphins, Mila?

There is no time before the dolphins.

Doctor Beck says, There is something you need to know. Many years ago a mother and two children were sent from a place called Cuba. They went on a small plane, the mother, a little girl, and a baby boy. The plane was lost at sea. We think the little girl on that plane was you.

Doctor Beck says, If this is true, your real name is Olivia. Your mother was American; your father is Cuban. The man we think is your father sent you a letter. Would you like me to read it to you?

I stand at the window and listen.

> *My dear Olivia,*
>   *There is so much to tell you. I don't know how to begin. I have a new family. We live in a small apartment in Havana.*
>   *Sadly, I am not free to come to the States to visit you. Nor, I'm afraid, are you permitted to come back to me. I am sorry. I must wait to hear from your American doctors and the American and Cuban governments about what I am to do next.*
>   *Until then I will look forward to the time when I see my little dolphin girl.*
>   *Yours sincerely,*
>   *Papi*

Inside, I am shaking.

Sandy says, Mila, if you are this girl, you have a father, you have family.

I don't remember this Papi.

I know only that family is people you love and care for, people who love and care for you. Who is this man who lives in a place where he cannot leave and I cannot come?

Sandy stands so close. I can smell her good smell. It is a smell of salt and sweet fruit.

I say, Sandy is family. Doctor Beck is family. Shay is family. Who is this Papi? I don't know. I only know I want to stay here with you.

Sixteen

Doctor Beck plays new music today. Not just the music of the man named Winter. Doctor Beck has different music. The music is of a man named Mozart. The music of Mozart is great, so great like the sea. It is everywhere with many voices all at once. It is a long story and many stories. It changes as it goes. More and more is in the music. It is not simple like the Winter music. It is big.

I listen to the music of Mozart. I feel in every little place inside me the music of Mozart.
I say, How can anyone make such music?
Is it that I can know Mozart and he can show me how he makes this music?

Doctor Beck says, Mozart is dead.

I am confused. I can hear this music so alive, but Mozart is dead?

Doctor Beck says, Mozart wrote the music a very long time ago. Mila, a writer writes a book, an artist paints a picture, a person makes a thing and sometimes, if the thing is very special, it is saved. It lasts. It lasts longer than the person who made the thing. It is kept alive by others even after the person who made it is dead.

That is what we're doing here, Mila. You and me. We are making something that will last beyond us. What we are doing will not fade like a sunset. It will not wash away like the waves on the sand.

I remember the sunset. I remember the waves on the sand. This remembering makes a feeling so big inside me.

I say, Each sunset, each wave is something to see once and never again. Is that not special too?

Doctor Beck looks at me, and I think I am saying something wrong. I want only to say right things. I want Doctor Beck to be happy.

Doctor Beck says, Yes, the sunset is important too.

Doctor Beck looks at me. I see excitement in her. I feel excitement in her.

She says, Mila, would you like to learn music like the music of Mozart? It is just another language. Like the language of English.

Sandy is watching Doctor Beck.

Doctor Beck says, We can teach you the language of music, Mila.

I take the hand of Doctor Beck. I like learning language very much. I want to learn everything Doctor Beck wants to show me.

Doctor Beck says, Sometimes human language and music language come together to make a song.

I know songs. I sing for Doctor Beck and Sandy a little song from the Winter tape.

Doctor Beck asks, Who taught you to sing like that, Mila?

I say, I teach me. The little song is so good in my ears, I listen again and again until I know it.

My singing makes Doctor Beck happy. Sandy is happy too. They are happy in different ways. They want to hear the song again, and I sing for them.

Then they teach me a song. A lullaby. A lullaby is a song for the baby to hear when it goes to sleep. The lullaby they teach me is about a baby all alone in a meadow. It makes me sad. The baby is all alone.

But the song is very pretty. I sing with Sandy and Doctor Beck. When all three, we, sing together, I feel good.

When I go to the sea, I will take this music with me.

The dolphins can like human music, I think.

Seventeen

Doctor Beck brings a present. It is hiding inside pretty paper. I take the paper off. Inside is an instrument for making music. Doctor Beck calls it a recorder, but it is different from the recorder that plays the tapes.

Sandy has a tight voice. She asks if I am learning too much at once. Sandy says maybe I can learn the music language after I learn better the English language.

But Doctor Beck says I need good work with my hands.
Doctor Beck says this is a right time to give different language.
Doctor Beck shows me how to take the recorder in my hands. She shows me where to blow.

I blow the recorder. I make a sound. EEEE! EEEE! EEEE! A bad sound comes, like angry birds.

Doctor Beck says not to worry. She says Doctor Peach can help me to learn.

The recorder is so pretty. Like the sea when it is white with foam. I touch the recorder with my human fingers. I take it along with my dolphin boots in my bed to sleep. Its skin is smooth. I stroke it and remember the inside of a shell.

Eighteen

Everyone is sleeping. I stand at the window. The light of the moon touches the river. I put my ear to the cold glass and I listen to the music of the water.

I am alone.

I am alone like the baby in the lullaby with the birds and the butterflies around him.

The wind makes the trees to sing. The wind makes the river to sing.

I sing too. I sing a gray song. A little, little Mila song. Not big, not many voices. Only one voice. A song of alone.

I think Justin hears my song. His bed squeaks and squeaks again and then one more time. I wait for his footsteps in the hallway. I wait for him to come and sit in the corner of my room.

He does not come.

It is late. Too late even for the man who comes to clean at night.

I open the door and go from my bedroom, down the stairs. I shut off the switches and turn the locks the way Sandy does when we go out. I go from the house and cross the big street to the river. I am afraid to go in the dark water, but I sense not danger there.

The water sings in my ears. I feel the pull of the sea. I swim a long time. I swim very far. The cold water empties the strength from my bones.

Again and again I make my dolphin name in my nose, but there is no answer.

I cannot find the warm sea where the dolphins wait. It is too far, and I am too alone.

It is hard to swim back. So hard. I am tired.

Nineteen

I am very sick. My breathing is not good.
I am taken to a hospital. All white. All the people in white. They give me medicine. I sleep and sleep.
They make something to help me breathe.
In my head I hear music. It is soft and good, like a mother singing. She is singing a lullaby. Her voice is high and sweet. I am searching for her.
I climb out of the sea, sand sticks to my legs. There is no mother here. I am lost.

Twenty

I feel bad, but not too bad.
Today I am in my own bed in my room at the house by the river. I am getting better.

Doctor Troy brings Shay to visit.

Shay stands by my bed, but she looks at the wall.

I take her hand.
I ask, Why, Shay, why do you look at the wall?

Shay does not answer.

The eyes of Shay are empty.
Where is Shay? I ask. Shay is not inside here.
I stroke the hand of Shay. I stroke the face of Shay. Shay, come back.

And she does. A little. I feel the push of her cheek into my open hand.

Doctor Troy says, Shay wants to do good work, but the work is so hard for her. She likes it best when you help her, Mila.

Doctor Beck says it is time for you to rest, Mila. Shay must go.

Shay holds my hand very hard.

Doctor Troy says, Say good-bye to Mila, Shay. He opens the hand of Shay, one finger, then one finger, then one finger, and takes the little hand of Shay.
Together they walk out of my room.

Twenty-one

I put on the warm clothes. I walk with Sandy. We cross the big street and go to the river. I know now the river is not a place for me to swim.

I see many houses on the bank of the river. From one house there is music. I say, Can we go to that house?

Sandy says, No. She says, We don't know the people who live there. You can't just go anywhere you wish, Mila. No person can come on the land of another without permission.

In the sea we go where we wish. We eat what we wish. We swim and play together in the big sea. Families of dolphin come together, from the cold sea, from the warm sea, from the deep sea and the cays. We play and sleep and eat together. We fight only the hungry ones who like to eat us. Sometimes the boy dolphin is pushing a girl dolphin. But most of the time the dolphins are so good with other dolphins. And we are going everywhere in the sea.

Sandy says, What about territory? Do dolphins have territory?

I ask, What is territory?

Sandy says, Territory is a place where you belong, a place belonging to you.

I think she means the place we like to go best. But we are not told we can go only there. We go there because we like to go there. No other reason. We share the good places with all who come.

I feel sad for humans. Humans go only where it

is permission. In the sea there are no locks or switches, no doors or walls.

Sometimes there are nets. Nets are death to dolphins. Nets are like walls in the sea.

Twenty-two

Sandy is my friend. She is worried.

I say not to worry. I am so happy. I love the lessons. I love my work with the computer. With the cards. With the paper and crayons and pencils and paint. We dance. We sing. We go different places. We swim. We play games. We have a good time all day. And I am so happy to be with Shay. I want Shay to make progress.

I sit on the classroom floor with Shay. I play a song on the recorder for her. Not a big song. Just three notes put together in a little pattern. I play it over and over. I play it soft for Shay. I play it loud for Shay. I put the recorder on the cheek of Shay and play very, very gentle. I hold the notes, and I can feel them rubbing against each other inside the recorder and inside me.

Listen, Shay, I say, and I face her with my recorder. I play so that the hair on the head of Shay lifts and falls with each note, so softly, like the wings of the ray flying through the slow green water.

I feel the music inside me. It says something more than just the notes, more than just the sounds. It is hearing with more than the ears. Like the way it is when I am with the dolphins. Or when I see Justin and Doctor Beck together. Or when Sandy talks about her father who is dead. There is a way I feel when Sandy hugs me so good and long and her stiff hair brushes my ear and her good smell fills my nose.

The music makes these different feelings inside me, too.

Shay stands and hops around the classroom.

She is making a funny kind of singing all by herself. It is a little, little thing like my three-note song on the recorder, but it makes Doctor Beck and Sandy and Doctor Troy happy. It makes me happy too.

Twenty-three

I can play five notes on the recorder. With those notes I can make many, many songs. It is not big music like the music Sandy gives me to put in the tape machine, it is not the music of Mozart, but my teacher, Doctor Peach, says if I can play these songs, I can play songs more harder in a little time.

I have to learn many notes before I can make music like Mozart. I want to play the recorder day and night. When I am not playing, I feel a tightness inside me, like when the sea grass catches my feet and I cannot break free. All around me swims the big music, but I am trapped inside the sea grass of my little notes.

Sandy is helping with my journal. My journal is this writing I do on the computer. Sandy shows me how much I learned in this year. She says when she first saw me, I knew five words. Now I know many words. But many words I do not know. And sometimes I make mistakes with the words I do know.

Doctor Beck makes more games for me to play. Other doctors come too. I like to play their games. When I understand what the doctors want, I am happy to do it. It makes the doctors happy too. I like to make the doctors happy too. Shay does not like the games so much. I help her. I show her how to play.

Shay sits on the floor. She looks at the wall. I see a look of lost in her eyes. I stroke the hair of Shay. I talk to Shay sometimes in dolphin, with my nose sound. Shay laughs at dolphin talk. I want to make Shay laugh all the time. But Doctor Beck says to make only human talk with her. So she can learn.

Shay is not happy. She can make only a little talk. One word. One word. One word.

Sandy says Shay never laughed before I came. Sandy says I am very smart to make Shay laugh with my dolphin talk. In the beginning, I did not make dolphin talk for Shay to laugh. I thought Shay understood dolphin talk. I thought Shay was like me. But Shay was not understanding dolphin talk, because I was not saying funny things and still Shay was laughing. So I know she is laughing because dolphin talk makes in her ears something funny. I love the sound of Shay laughing.

There is so much laughing in my dolphin family. Inside laugh. Outside laugh. I laugh with Sandy, but I miss dolphin laughing. I ask, Sandy, do you have a tape of dolphin laughing?

Sandy says no, but she will look for this tape.

Justin brings me a radio.
He says, This is old. My father sent me a new one. You can have this.
Justin shows me to fit the plug in the little wall holes.

You turn it on here, he says. And move the knob to tune the stations.

Justin shows me where to put my hand.

I turn the radio off and on. If I move the knob so slow, I can find music, so much music hiding in the radio. If I turn the knob and turn the knob, I can find so many different sounds. So many different voices. There is so much inside the radio. And it is all human.

Twenty-four

I know seven notes on the recorder now. G-A-B-C-D-F-E. I play so many songs. They go up a little, down a little, like small waves on a calm day. It makes me happy to play the songs again and again.

Doctor Beck and the other doctors make the games hard for me. They say I learn fast. They say I can catch up with others my age before too long. Good. I want to catch up. I want to be with others.

I chase Shay around outside, the way I chased my dolphin cousins. But Shay stands in one place and I catch her too easy. Shay drops to the ground. She does not like when I move fast.

I throw Shay a ball, very gentle. She does not

put her hands out to catch it. I put the ball in her hands. She drops it. She has two good hands. My dolphin family, they would like to have the hands of Shay.

Shay uses her hands to eat. Only to eat.

I love to use my hands. To play the games, to make the music on the recorder. To make the machine with the tapes play. To bring the music from the radio. To make the computer say the words I am thinking. I like every little thing I am learning with my fingers and my toes.

Twenty-five

Sandy has a bag in her hand. In the bag she has many books. I like books, but you cannot read them in the water. Yesterday I took one book with me in the bath and the book looked very bad after. I am learning. Some things can go in the water, like my dolphin boots, but other things, like books, are not so good when they get wet.

Sandy says, Remember, Mila. Don't go swimming with these.
Sandy thinks I need help to remember, but I remember many things.

Sometimes I even remember a little before the dolphin time. I remember sitting on the knees of a woman. I remember a game of riding her knees.

I am drawing for Sandy a picture of riding the knees.

I ask, Does Shay remember the time before Doctor Troy and Doctor Beck?

Sandy says it is hard to know. The mother of Shay did not talk to her. She kept Shay in a little room all day, all night. For Shay it was always dark.

I miss the bright light of the ocean, the good bright light of dolphin time. I am too sad to think of Shay always in the dark.

And in the sea, a dolphin mother always is making certain her baby is good. A dolphin aunt is always near to help. The baby has food to eat, sometimes the thick fishy milk from the dolphin mother, sometimes the sweet fish fresh from the sea. The baby is protected when a shark comes. Where is the good mother to protect Shay?

Doctor Beck says not all humans are good. She

says, Even good humans are not good all the time, Mila. But most humans want to be good. Doctor Beck asks, Are all dolphins good?

I do not know how to answer this.
I ask Doctor Beck, Tell me what it means to be good.

My question makes Doctor Beck tired. I see it in her hands. I see it when she moves.
Doctor Beck says, Good is honest, good is fair, good is doing what is right.

I think dolphins are good. Not all of the time, but most of the time. Maybe dolphins are not so different from humans.

Twenty-six

Doctor Beck is happy today. She says, Mila, your journal is very beautiful. Very important. She says my writing is good science. Doctor Beck asks me to write about my time in the sea. She wants to know dolphin life. She wants to learn dolphin talk! She says to know these things will be a most important learning for people.

I look at Doctor Beck.
For one moment, she makes me think of the orca who is so big and strong and beautiful, and so dangerous when he is hungry. I think for one moment that Doctor Beck is hungry to eat me. Then I think, Doctor Beck is not an orca.

Doctor Beck, I say. Dolphin knowing is so big. I do not have all the outside words to tell you.

But Doctor Beck wants to know very strong about the dolphin time. If you could teach us what you've learned, Mila . . . there is nothing more important you could do.

❖

*I come from the sea. I come from the deep tons, from
the ringing bubbles, from the clicking claws and
rolling tides. I come from the many winds of the sea,
from the place between sky and deep where the gulls
cry and the waves shift under the bright eye of the
sun. On clear nights the round moon leans across the
sea. Its arm stretches, scooping water. The moon
paints a stripe of light. My dolphin mother swims in
the path of the moon. I am not like her. I have hands
at the ends of my arms, fingers at the ends of my
hands. My fingers open and close. With them I do
things the others cannot. I am not like the others. I
have feet. I can walk on land. The dolphin moves like
light. The dolphin flies through the wet breath of
the sea. I cannot swim the quiet stroke of the dolphin. I cannot hear the whole sound, though it sings
through me.*

*Each morning I swim out to them. We brush
through the water, feeding, playing, singing, resting,*

dancing in the rolling waves, racing from storms, racing for the joy of moving with the water slipping over our backs, with the water sliding under our chins. The water opens, and we dive in through the wild paths of the sea.

In the sea there is always play. Anything and everything is to chase and catch and toss and taste and drag. There are near crashes and laughter, dolphin laughter, sparkling like a thousand drops of sunlight. My dolphin cousins play with me gently. I am so little beside them. They know me inside and out. I lick my lips as they send their humming through me. I never tire of the thrill as they slide up under my fingers or I glide down over their flukes.

At birth times, I can sense the change, the humming aimed at one, and all of us begin the wait. It is exciting, the waiting before a calf is born. The squeaks, the creaks and clickings, the chirps and whistles. Nothing is the same as we wait with the waiting mother. She bends and stretches, bends and stretches. She claps her flukes against ocean swells and the sound travels through my bones.

We wait for new life to slip, tail first, into the big sea.

I watch the others, seeing, hearing, feeling what they feel. My dolphin mother touches me, one stroke of her flipper, telling me when it is time.

Sinking below the surface, eyes open, I see there, in a cloud of pink, a tail, then a body and head, coming from the slit in the underbelly of the mother.

A quick spin and the cord snaps and slowly, what is not dolphin, what is not calf, mixes with the sea and drifts down through the deep blue. And what is left is a new cousin.

The mother guides it to the surface, but the calf knows what to do, and breaking through to the air takes a first gasp through the top of its head.

The calf is wrinkled from being folded inside its mother, its tail curls like an underwater weed, opening slowly with the gentle tug of the tide.

The calf bumps against its mother, searching.

The mother studies her calf, stroking it. They nuzzle, skin to skin. The mother hums, sounding her baby, inside and out, while the calf pokes its new self along the length of its mother, until the mother rolls on her side and the calf finds milk, a great stream of thick, sweet milk, rushing reward for the pressure of lips.

Sometimes the birth does not go right and the baby dies. And then the mother lifts her silent calf to the air, but there is no calf there, only an empty body, and the mother tells a story, about this thing that happened, and the others join in telling their parts, and the story grows for days and days until the mother is ready to let the baby go.

When I came, in a storm, my dolphin mother had given birth. Her dolphin baby did not blow and did not blow. Tenderly, she let her dead calf go, and reached for me.

She stood the storm, the sharp rain stinging her hide; she carried me, alive, through the giant swells to the cay, where I woke the next day to a calmer sea, and a warming sun, and a new life.

When I was so little and hungry, my dolphin mother stroked me and, leaving her white underside showing there above her flukes, she gave me her milk.

I gulped and choked, gulped and choked, gulped and swallowed and choked some more, but swallowed enough to grow strong and stronger and finally fat and warm on the fishy richness of dolphin milk.

Each day my dolphin family dives for fish, I stay swimming above. Sometimes I swim a little away.

When my aunt catches me, she claps her jaw, slaps water at me with her tail. But I need to always move in the deep water. I drift away from my aunt, floating between the new mothers and their calves. The tingle of their soundings passes through me.

My dolphin mother returns, a fish sideways in her mouth. She locks down with her pointed teeth and the tail and head fall away, down, down through the darkness. She flips out a fish for me to eat. I take the fish in my hands, my good hands for stroking dolphin backs, for holding, and tearing, and throwing, and pulling. I catch the fish in my good hands and tear into its sweet flesh with my teeth.

In the night, things rise from the deep. They rise with their long arms, with their sharp beaks, with their strong suckers to pull me under and hold me until I have no breath. I struggle in a blinding cave of pain. My dolphin mother hears and comes, ramming the monster that holds me, and the others ram it too. They batter and bang the beast until I am free, then carry me near shore, where I crawl onto the sand and remember to breathe.

I sleep there on the beach until I can make sea again. After that I sleep always on the rocks, alone.

In the light I am not afraid of the deep, of the darkness close beneath me, but at night the deep frightens me. My dolphin mother understands, my dolphin family understands. As the day stills and the light dims and the sun melts into a pool of spreading red, the sea quiets and we turn toward the nearest cay and I climb from the sea, trailing weeds and long ribbons of grass strung over my shoulders and through my hair. I make a nest for myself with my good hands, pulling wide leaves around me. I make a nest for my lonely sleep and wrap myself in my long, long hair, and give myself to the dark while always within reach, I hear the sound of my family breathing, blowing softly offshore, waiting for morning.

Sometimes it is good to be on land, to be alone. In the sea there is the always touching, the always talking, the always moving. Sometimes I like the quiet. I like the feel of land under my feet. But most times it is dolphin company inside and outside that feels so good.

Sometimes, in the day, sharks will come. They are simple, those sharks. They are simple as rocks. When they come, my family knows what to do. They take turns swimming very fast, and one by one, bang, they smash into the shark, catching it on the side. And after a crash or two or three the shark will swim slowly away, no fights, no bites. But sometimes the shark drops down, down, out of sight, through the gloom where a thousand blind eyes, where a thousand hungry mouths, wait below in the dark for supper to drift past.

But the orca is not simple like the shark. The orca is quick like a stick of lightning. Sometimes the orca can be near and it is safe. I will watch him, beautiful black and white, bold swimmer, big, brave brother, but sometimes the orca will come thinking to eat dolphins, and when he comes thinking that, he always does. And then the ocean has a different feel, and there is fear, and flight and struggle, and in the end sadness, and there is a new song to sing about the dolphin who was and is no more, about the orca who came hungry and ate a brother. And for a while everything is different in the sea. The sound is different, the taste is different. Until the difference becomes part of the long song.

The old ones, they can tell when the orca is hungry, when it is not. They know the blow of a whale, miles at sea, and the beat of a ship cutting through the open *waves. They know the sound of the sun rising out of the sea and setting again back into it.*

The sea is a living music, it is the whisper of fish, the roar of wind, the chatter of stones and sand, of weeds and reefs in the wave-churned surf. It is all music.

My cousins call to each other and run over the waves, curving out, dropping back, a fast and springing dance. They rise, gleaming, the sun leaping off their shining skin, and they stand on their tails, all together, moving with one mind, with one song, with one motion. At night, from the rocks, I watch them at their feeding. I watch them at their play. They are lit by a shining glow, everything washed in green light against the dark. My dolphin family in their night-fire clothes, their mouths glowing as they open into the shining tide. All the time talking inside each other, outside each other.

I understand, though I cannot say all; still, I understand everything when I look in their eyes, when I feel the stroke of their ripe skin against mine. I understand in their speed or their slowness, in their leaping or their diving, in their roughness or their calm.

I cannot swim as fast, I cannot swim as smooth. My cousins know I am different. The water knows I am different. Always the water asks if I would like to come deep and deeper. But once I went too deep, and it hurt in my ears and my eyes and my nose, and my throat shut and my chest burst and my skin broke with needles of pain while my head exploded. And my dolphin mother knew that if I lived, I must not go deep again, and so I run beside her, or atop her or between her and an aunt. I ride with a cousin or a sister and I am never left behind. This is how my dolphin family cares for me. If they are eating, if they are playing, they look inside each other and know what is needed and together what they must do.

Things float by. Things from the human world. Bottles and jars and plastic jugs. Sometimes a cousin swallows a glass ball or gets tied up in line. And then there is sadness and the dolphin mothers carry the young ones, holding their soft gray bodies up to the air to blow. Sometimes with my fingers I can do what must be done and pull the ball from the throat of my cousin so he can eat again or untangle the line from his tail so he can swim, and then my cousin lives. But sometimes he dies, and we wait for the mother to let go, to give her baby to the deep, where it drifts down into the blue below and drops away forever.

The old ones do not eat such dangerous things, but young ones do not know. I have eaten fish dead too long, fish dying, filled with poison, sick fish slow enough to be caught by me.

On the cays, too, I have eaten things that made my stomach wild with pain, I have eaten things that come leaping back up, rushing past my burning throat, out through my open mouth. When I do this, I am not strong enough to swim, and my dolphin mother and my dolphin aunt carry me. The sea makes a soft bed to rest my hurting stomach in, but sometimes the smallest movement makes me sick and I am too weak even to be in the sea, and then my mother and my aunt and my cousins and the old ones wait for me.

Sometimes on the big cay, men come. They have machines. They have guns. They frighten me. My dolphin family stays far from shore when men are there, and I sleep on a different cay where no plane can land and no man can find a place of comfort.

The men who come to the big cay sometimes leave food and water and things I like. But I stay there only when the men are away. Once the cay was quiet and I came on the land, but one man was left. He slept in a pool of his own blood and did not breathe and it frightened me. I ran back into the sea and we swam to the north and I slept on the rocks and we did not go back to the big cay for a very long time. Instead I stayed on the bits of land too small for a man to camp and sleep but bursting with life and big enough for me.

We travel from cay to cay. And on each I find a different comfort. On one is a trickle of fresh water flowing, on another are pools in the pockets of rocks; a third has grasses and roots sweet and filling, and pools of salt water, with food left by the tide.

Some times are quiet. We leave the group, old ones come, some aunts and cousins. The pace is slower, calmer. But sometimes our group joins with other groups, and then there is great leaping, squeaking, clicking, tail dancing, wave driving, bubble churning, mounds of us, different colors, different sizes, different shapes, but all one family in the big sea, the big sea big enough for all the chirping, laughing, fast, and humming dolphins. Then it is so good to watch, to feel the strong singing inside me.

When the dolphin groups gather, there are stories, there is joy. We jump the waves, and race, and chase the darting fish. And sometimes the boys fight or chase a girl and then the sea churns and inside my stomach twists like a tight net biting into the tender parts of me, but the next day all is good again and the dolphins are friends, and if that cannot be, then the angry ones go and the rest play on.

There is never a time when my ears want for song or sound, when inside or out, along my skin, or inside my bones, I want for anything. And although I cannot stand on my tail or jump the waves, although I cannot catch the fish or slide in silence through the sea, although I cannot understand the fast voice or the deep stories, I am a part of the long song. I sing my own funny clicking, chirping, squeaking story, and the story is good.

Twenty-seven

A television is another world where everything is small and everyone and everything is trapped behind a wall of glass. The people of the television world cannot come in the world with us. They live behind a wall you can see through, like the glass in my door. I think sometimes they will come through like when dolphins jump from the water. But they never do. Maybe it is dangerous for them to come into our world because they are so small.

The people in the television have music all around them. I like the music. The music helps them to live behind the wall, but maybe they do not always hear the music. They are like Shay. The music is in their ears, but it does not touch them. I feel sad that they cannot get out, that they cannot escape.

The television has fast words, very fast, faster than the radio. I have trouble to understand everything I see and hear.

In that television I see a girl with long, long hair. She is not wearing clothes. She is on a beach. I am interested to see a girl on the beach. I watch. Then she is not on the beach. She is in a new place, wrapped in a blanket. A hand offers the girl a drink. The girl sees the water in a cup, but she is not certain what to do. First her finger dips in the water. Then her finger goes to her mouth. The girl decides the water is good to drink, and she makes a cup with her hands. She does not know to drink from the paper cup. She drinks water poured from the cup into her hands. The girl is very short. Her ears are very big.

Then I see Doctor Beck and Sandy inside the television. They are with the little big-ear girl. They are trapped in the television with her.

I run to the television to help Sandy and Doctor Beck get out. I beat the television with my shoulder. I cannot make the wall to come down. I take my chair. I throw my chair at the television. Lights flash everywhere. I jump away. Little lights snapping and popping. Then the lights are gone. But Doctor Beck and Sandy are gone too.

I run. I run everywhere in the big house, asking help! Help!

A door opens. Doctor Beck is there, and she is big again. She is in a room next to the television room. She is there with the other doctors. They sit in a room I could never see before. I run my hands over Doctor Beck, so happy she is free, that she is safe. I stroke her arms and her face and her hair.

Where is Sandy?

Doctor Beck says, Sandy is right here.

I see Sandy. She is big again too. She sits apart from the others. Her back is turned to me.

Sandy is crying. I know how the inside feels when there is crying. I run to Sandy. I am so happy she is not trapped in the world of the television anymore.

Doctor Troy says, She did not recognize herself.

They look at me like I am stupid like a shark.

Why do they look at me this way?

Twenty-eight

I do not sleep. I watch out the window. I think about what Doctor Troy said.

She did not recognize herself.

I know he talked about me.

I remember the girl on the television. I remember each place she went. It is like remembering the notes of a song. I cannot forget that big-ear girl, the girl with Sandy and Doctor Beck. I look at my reflection in the mirror. There is a thin face, brown skin, short hair.

Doctor Troy said, She did not recognize herself. He must be wrong. I was not in the television. I could not be in that little life behind the glass and this big life all at the same time. Unless the life behind the glass is a remembering. Can they reach inside me and take a remembering? When I first came here, Doctor Beck put many wires on my head and told me to sleep. Did she take my rememberings then? I am so confused. The girl behind the glass, the girl with long hair, the place where she stood made me think of the rocks where I drank the freshwater, the cay where I ate from the tide pools.

I think about the girl, naked. Her hair so long and black. Her skin gray and white with streaks of salt. And her little circle scars.

I look in the mirror again. There are the big ears, the big, big ears. There are the little scars.

Doctor Troy said, She did not recognize herself.

The girl was me! Mila.

I am afraid. I saw the girl with no clothes. I

thought, This is a bad girl. She has no clothes. I saw her long wild hair. I thought, This girl is ugly with her long wild hair. I saw the girl with her eyes showing white. I thought, This girl has fear. I thought, I am happy not to be that girl.

But I am that girl.

That is what Doctor Troy meant.

The remembering of my capture is taken out of my head and put behind the glass of the television. If they have that, do they have all my other rememberings too? But how could they take my rememberings when I still have them? My head feels like it is caught in the claw of a crab.

I need to know. I need someone to help me understand. Shay cannot help.

Who can help me?

Twenty-nine

There is a man who works in the house to make it clean. He has a face of lines. There are long thin eels under the skin of his hands. They move as he works.

The man comes up the steps at night when we are to sleep. He cleans the classroom and the offices, he washes the bathrooms and the floors and walls. His sound is different from the others in the house. I like to watch him. The man is quiet. Like the little diggers that tunnel into the sand. So, so quiet.

The man does not look through my window. He looks at the floor when he cleans in front of my room. Only the floor.

Why does the man not look at me?

In the quiet night, he carries his mop past my room and the handle hits my door. I am making a little song on my recorder. The mop sounds like knocking. I put my recorder down. I think maybe the man wants to play with me. I want to play all the time. But Doctor Beck and Sandy and Shay and the others, they are all sleeping at night in their rooms. This man has with him water. He uses it to make all the floor shining like the wet skin of my dolphin mother.

When I come to the door, the man looks up for only a moment. His head is down, his shoulders down, but he lifts his eyes to me. There is something in his eyes that hurts inside me. He turns away from my door and suddenly he is falling over his bucket, making it spill on the floor. He makes a sound like the dolphin in trouble.

I try to open the door to go to the man. To help him. The door will not open. I am trapped inside the glass of the door. It is like the television. I cannot come out. I beat my hands on the glass. I beat my hands on the locked door. I beat my hands until my blood comes.

I beat against the glass, against the wall, against the window.

Justin comes. He yells through the door at me to stop.

I look at my hands that held the fin of my dolphin mother. My hands bleed.

Doctor Beck comes and opens the door. She looks at me. She says, What were you thinking?

I don't know. I don't know what I am thinking. But I am alone. I am trapped in the net of the room. In the net of humans. I think maybe I am drowning in the net of humans.

Thirty

I sit in my room. Doctor Beck examines my hands. She says words. She pours a thousand words on me.

The man who makes the floor clean has fear of me. Do they all have fear of me? They lock me in a room and do not let me free.

In my dolphin family I was free. Now I have a locked door.

I do not understand why they lock me in. I am not like the orca who goes after the dolphin, who runs the dolphin down and eats the dolphin. I am not like a net to trap the dolphin and hold the dolphin down so she cannot breathe. I am happy to play. I am happy to swim in the little pool. I am happy to talk their talk, to make their music. I do not know why they lock me in.

I try to learn the language of humans. I try to think the way of humans. Each day I have more words to say my thoughts. But I do not have enough words for what I feel now.

Sandy stands at the edge of my room. She does not look at me. She looks at Doctor Beck. She looks at Doctor Beck a long time with no words.

I think of the sea and my other life. I remember my body sliding through the silk of the sea, riding between the silk body of my mother and the silk body of my aunt. I think of playing with my dolphin cousins, of the sea singing and singing.

I want to go there. I need to go there.

Please let me go there.

Doctor Beck looks away.

Sandy says, What have we done?

Thirty-one

Sandy comes to my room. She touches the bandages on my hands. She is all sadness, in her eyes, in her walk.

Why do you keep me in a locked room?

Sandy says, Your room has been locked for a long time. Since the night you went swimming in the Charles River, Mila.

I did not know this. I did not know.
I tell her, I will not go in the river again. I promise. Please unlock the door.

Sandy says, We can't.

I ask, Why? Why do you have to lock me in?

Sandy says, When the government learned about your swim in the Charles, they were very angry with Doctor Beck. They wanted to know how she could let you get out. The government told Doctor Beck to keep you locked in or you would be given to someone else.

I ask, Why does the government talk this way about me?

Sandy says, They think they own you, Mila. Sandy says, Remember when we walked along the Charles and you heard music and wanted to go in the house and we talked about territory and property? Mila, you are government property.

No, I am Mila.

Sandy says, The government doesn't think of you as Mila. It thinks of you as an investment. It is paying your way, Mila. It wants to be sure no harm comes to you, no one hurts you. That you are protected.

Why is the government afraid harm will come to me? Does one human hurt the other?

Sandy says, When people don't understand a thing, it frightens them. There are some people so interested in you, they would take you away from us. There are other people who are just plain frightened of you. People who don't know you. The man who cleans the floor, Mr. Aradondo, and people outside, in the big world. They do not understand a girl who lived with dolphins. You are different, Mila. You look different, you sound different. But it isn't just the way you talk or walk. It isn't just the way you look. Your thinking is different. Mila, you think like a dolphin.

Sandy says, Humans see things only the human way. We look at the dolphin and we think it does not look human, it does not talk human, it does not act human. It must not be as good as human. Humans think they are the best, that they know the only right way.

I am confused. I know only this thing. I must have the door unlocked.

Sandy says, Someday the door will be unlocked. When you know the language, when you know the rules, the door will be unlocked.

When I know the language, when I know the rules, when they unlock the door, I can run back to the warm sea. I can leave my human clothes on the beach. I can leave my human thought on the beach. I will go home.

Thirty-two

I have decided to work very hard at being human so they will let me go free. My hands still hurt. I have a difficult time with my computer, but I try. I turn the volume off. I do not want to hear the computer talk. The sound is ugly. Like my voice.

There are spots on the walls from my blood. I cannot play the recorder with my hands wrapped. I am sorry I did this to my hands. Hands are gifts. I want to play the recorder. I can hear the music in my head. If I do not listen to Doctor Beck and Sandy and the others, I can hear the music. It is simple music. Five notes, seven notes. I want to make this little music. I try to use my fingers, but when I move them the blood starts again, and so I wait for my hands to heal.

Doctor Beck is happy to see me come to class

this morning. She asks, "Mila, would you like to play a new game?"

I play her games. I make progress. When I make progress, she is happy. She can give a good report to the government. And I can be free. When I know enough human, then I can return to the warm ocean, to my dolphin home.

Thirty-three

I ask to see the movie of myself that begins when the Coast Guard picked me up on the island. Now I recognize myself. I can feel the sand under my feet. I can feel the soft breath of winter sun on my skin. I can feel the thirst. My lips are cracked. My tongue is swollen. I do not miss the thirst.

I look at the girl on the island with her black hair. She looks like Shay . . . I look like Shay.

Doctor Beck shows me all the games we played when I first came. I remember how hard I tried to know what she wanted.

All the games are easy now. I can do them all.

In my room today Doctor Beck brings a man of plastic filled with air.

"Here is something new, Mila," Doctor Beck says. And she hits the man filled with air. She

hits him with her fist. The man drops backward, then pops back up in place.

"Now you hit him, Mila," Doctor Beck says.

I am not understanding.

Doctor Beck says, "When you feel angry or
afraid, you can hit him. You don't have to hit the
walls of your room, you don't have to hit the
door or the windows. If you feel angry or afraid,
you can hit *him*. Then no one is hurt. Do you
understand? You mustn't hurt yourself again."

I say, "Doctor Beck, why do you ask me to do
this? I do not feel danger from this man filled
with air. He is not like the hungry shark. He is
not like the orca. He is smiling. Why do you
ask me to hit this man who is smiling?"

Doctor Beck says, "Humans feel aggression,
Mila. Aggression is angry feelings. When you
hit the walls in your room the other night and
made your hands bleed, you felt aggression."

I do not understand this aggression. Only
the wish to be free. Only the wish to open the
door. I do not wish to hit a man filled with air.
This will not make me free.

Doctor Beck says, "It is better to hit this punching man than to hit the walls, Mila. It will not hurt your hands."

I say, "Doctor Beck, it is better to open the door. It is better to be free. Then I do not want to hit the walls. I want to think like human. I want to act like human. But I cannot do this thing. I have no need to hit the punching man. Please. Take him away."

Thirty-four

I made a song for the recorder. It is a song that swam over and over in my head all these days my hands were in bandages. It is made from the notes I know. I put the notes together to make music like dolphins doing slow swimming, brushing the waves, little jumps, little dives, swimming dolphin music.

"Listen," I say.

I play my song for Doctor Peach and Doctor Beck and Doctor Troy and Shay and Sandy and Justin.

They are very quiet when they hear my song. It makes something happen inside them to hear this music. I can see, the way I see how the dolphins feel.

They don't say words when I finish, but I am seeing something in their eyes, I am seeing something in the way they move, I am hearing something inside them. And it is good.

Tonight I play the music for Mr. Aradondo, the man who cleans the house. I think maybe this making music can help him to be not afraid of me. I come to my door with my recorder and play for him. Drops of wet form on his lip and I taste something through the door, something not good.

I take the recorder down from my mouth and wipe it against my leg. I touch the glass. "Mr. Aradondo, don't be afraid."

He does not look at me.

I hit the door once with my flat palm to get his attention. Mr. Aradondo jumps.

He gathers his bucket and his mop and goes away, quickly. He does not finish the floor.

Thirty-five

I ask Sandy to stay after Doctor Beck goes.

I say, "Tell me about Shay. Why don't I see Shay anymore? We eat at different times. She does not come to the classroom. I miss her. How can we live in the same house and not see the other? Sometimes I hear her. I hear her sound. But I don't ever see her."

Sandy says, "Doctor Beck does not work with Shay anymore. She gave Shay to Doctor Troy."

I say, "How can she give Shay to anyone? Only Shay can give herself."

Sandy says, "You are right. Shay seems to understand that too. She is going deeper and deeper inside herself, Mila. She is locking herself away. We can hardly reach her anymore."

Shay is trapped the way I am trapped in this net of humans.

But I cannot go the way of Shay. There is too much to see and hear and feel and taste on the outside to live only on the inside.

Tomorrow we go to the tower with the television people so they can take more pictures of me. I know now. The television is not another world. It is only moving pictures. People are curious. They are curious to see many things. They are curious to see a dolphin girl. I understand curious. Dolphins are curious. When a boat comes, making its loud sound in the sea, dolphins come. The dolphin cousins want to see the humans, want to play, to swim with the boats.

Sandy says, "The more people know of you, the less fear they will have."

But what do people know of me? Only pictures on the television. Only words. I am a thing to look at, to play with. Not a thing to touch and care for.

Thirty-six

Justin comes to see me. He makes me happy. When I am with him, it is like being with a dolphin cousin or a dolphin brother. I like him very much. He makes his hair go back with his hand, like Doctor Beck, and watches me. He makes a soft sound between his lips. His teeth are very white. He is long in arms and legs and is moving all the time and many times, day and night, I think about swimming with him. His ears are small and pretty like the ears of Doctor Beck. I like his ears. Inside his clothes are strong bones. If Justin Beck was dolphin, I think he will be my mate. But he is not dolphin. And I am not human. Not human enough.

I ask if Justin will bring me to the Hump. The Hump is a place outside where you put your ear to a little hill of grass and listen to the sea.

Justin says to Doctor Beck, "I won't let her run away."

The world is busy outside. Across the noisy road the wind makes the river into a thousand ripples. New leaves, so green, are on the trees. The light grows stronger.

Justin sits with me on the grass, but not so close. Justin does not like to be so close. Not to me, not to Doctor Beck. In that way he is so different from the dolphin.

Justin asks, "What was it like, Mila? Living in the sea." His voice is soft and rumbly, like the deep earth moving.

I say, "I can give a long answer. It is like a many hundred things. I can ask you what it is like living on the land. You can talk and talk all day. You can talk many days about all the little things there are and not say it all. Do you understand?"

Justin says, "Yes."

I say, "Some days rain comes, some days wind comes. Some days there is no drink. Some days no food. But always the dolphins are together."

Justin says, "All those years. How did you do it?"

I watch a boy and a girl walking, hands touching, shoulders touching, so good, so close. I look at Justin with the little ears, with the white teeth. Beautiful human boy. I say, "I did what the dolphins did. I went where the dolphins went. It was not hard. I did not know another thing to do."

Justin runs his hand over the grass. "You must hate this. Being inside all the time. My mother telling you what to do. She thinks you can teach her to talk with dolphins. That's all I ever hear about these days."

I feel many signals from Justin Beck. I sense something, but I do not understand it. He has a need to be close, but it is not me he wants.

I look and look at his hand moving in the grass.

Justin says, "Do you ever get tired of all the attention?"

I say, "I like to play, and to talk, and to all the time do things with my hands and go places and see what I have not seen and hear what I have not heard. Sometimes people are so good to me, people I do not know. They give me things when they see me. They send me things."

Justin says, "I don't know how you do it. I can't imagine what it would be like to live on land with your family one day and then be part of a dolphin pod the next. And then all of this. Do you remember any of the past, the plane crash or your mother . . . ?"

My heart goes very loud inside me. I cannot make words.

Red comes to the face of Justin. "Hey, Mila, I'm sorry. Why would you want to remember that? I hate thinking about my family splitting, and that wasn't anywhere near as bad as what happened to you."

I am on this beach of grass with no ocean, with no quiet, with no clean air to breathe. The wind is cool. My ears hurt. The song of the ocean roars inside the Hump. Justin's questions stir up feelings I don't understand.

I ask, "Justin, where is the ocean I am hearing? Where is it? Is it under the grass?"

Justin says, "It's really just the cars driving past us on Storrow Drive, the sound of their wheels inside the Hump. It's a pretty crummy excuse for the sea."

Listening, I imagine the real sea. A gull cries overhead.

Justin says, "Mila, are you okay?"

I say, "Justin, I want to go back where the warm food hides in the tide pools. I want to go back to the sea, where I do not feel the crushing of my heart by the ideas in my head."

I am afraid what Justin will think, that he will be angry with me. Yet he is not angry. He listens.

"But if I do go back, Justin, I am the dolphin girl, the girl you laugh at."

Justin says, "I am not laughing, Mila. I wish I could go back sometimes too."

"Justin, I think about tomorrow and tomorrow always locked in my room, or the classroom, wearing clothes, eating dead food. I want to go back. To my dolphin family, to my dolphin home." I wrap my arms around myself. I shut my eyes and let the sounds come inside me.

Justin sits at my side. He does not tell me what to do like Sandy or Doctor Beck. He does not treat me the way the doctors treat me. He does not look another place when I say a thing he does not like. He listens. He treats me the way we treat the new dolphin who comes to swim with us.

Justin says, "My mother won't let you go."

I say, "What if she keeps me locked here forever? Always to play the little games, always looking for dolphin talk? What if I do all she asks and I am still not good enough?"

Justin says, "You're already good enough. You can do so much more than anyone ever thought. But they don't know when to stop. Especially not my mother."

He looks out over the Charles River. "My mother likes to be in control. It's hard for her when she's not in control. She can't control me. She can control you. That's why you're her little darling right now. Why you're her pet. But you don't have to let her do all this to you, Mila. You don't have to do everything she says. You don't have to make her happy. You couldn't.

Believe me. I know from experience. Nothing can make her happy."

I feel anger in him. A small eye of anger. But it is mostly liking I sense in Justin. I turn to Justin. I am listening to the sound of his heart. I am listening to the signals he sends. I see the white teeth, the beautiful ears. With this human I am most happy. With this human I am most sad.

Thirty-seven

I ask Doctor Beck not to lock my room anymore. "I will not run away," I tell her. "I need to come and to go, like the rest of you. Do you understand?"

Doctor Beck stares at me. For a moment she sees me, not as a subject for her research, she really sees me. And then the open eyes shut again. But maybe not all the way.

"And the classroom too," I say. "And the front door. No more locked doors, Doctor Beck."

She explains to me about her money from the government. How the government has rules she must follow. How her job is to protect me. To keep me safe.

"Mila, it has to be this way."

She reminds me about the time I swam in the night river and how sick that made me. "You've never fully recovered from that. Your health is still fragile." She talks about gentle Mr. Aradondo, who refuses to clean the floor outside my room. "What would he say?"

"Doctor Beck, one time there was a dolphin who made life dangerous for the others. That dolphin was set apart to live alone. This is a very sad way for a dolphin. Dolphins love to be with other dolphins. Please do not set me apart anymore. I am not dangerous. I will teach you what I can, I will learn from you what I can, but you must unlock the doors. I will not play, I will not write in this journal, I will not eat, until you unlock the doors."

"Mila, be reasonable. You've been losing weight ever since you came to us. You can't stop eating."

I am not listening.

"Mila."

I am not listening.

"Mila!"

I AM NOT . . .

Thirty-eight

This morning, after nine days, I eat again, I speak again, I write in my journal again. This morning I leave my bed and sit in the chair by the open window. This morning Doctor Beck said, "Yes. I will unlock the door."

I ask to take the needle out of my arm, and Sandy brings me a little food from the kitchen.

Doctor Beck says, "Mila, I'm sorry it took so long. I put your case forward every day. Even now, they only gave permission to unlock your bedroom door. The door to the outside must still be locked. That was the best I could do. But you can go out anytime you like. You need only ask. Only remember. If anything happens to you, Mila, the government will never forgive me."

Justin says, "Way to go, Mila."

I have trouble remembering all the days when

I did not eat. I remember like a dream. Shay came. And Justin. Sandy played the videos of all my television stories and progress reports. I saw the wild girl with the curtain of salt-crust hair and the frightened eyes. I saw the eager girl with her hair cut, wearing clothes, struggling with words and cards and computers. I saw the girl who sat at a desk, drew pictures, played three notes on the recorder. The girl who looked almost human, acted almost human.

Mr. Aradondo is not afraid of me anymore. He looked through the window in my door each night. And last night he came inside my room, standing opposite Doctor Beck. He came all the way into my room and stared down at me where they had me tied to the bed so I wouldn't rip out the feeding tube. He stared at me a long time. In another language he spoke. Doctor Beck helped me to write his words on the computer. "*Tienes una fiebra alta. Her fever is so high. Her cheeks are two flames,*" he said.

Doctor Beck nodded, checking the feeding tube.

Mr. Aradondo said, "Mila, Doctor Beck needs you to eat. She needs you to take your medicine, child. *¿Me entiendes?* Do you understand?"

His words, his voice made me think of another time, another place. I remembered an old man who carried me on his shoulders and told me stories of Africa. A good man, who smelled like the earth.

"*Abuelo*," I whispered.

Mr. Aradondo's hand shook as he touched the top of my head. He had no more fear. Only sadness, great sadness, as he stared down at me.

Doctor Beck's mouth opened. "What did you say, Mila?"

I looked at the old man with his lined face and his kind eyes.

"*Abuelo*," I said.

Grandfather.

Thirty-nine

I am very weak, sitting in this chair, too weak to leave the room that is no longer locked. I can change my computer from Spanish to English. English to Spanish. I call up the picture of grandfather and remember my own *abuelo*.

Doctor Beck, I think she begins to understand. My smile is my own, it is something I give freely, because I want to give it. I am someone, the girl they call Mila, behind the smile. I think they begin to see. I think they begin to see me.

Several of the doctors on the team have gone away. The two-way mirror is closed now behind curtains.

But Doctor Beck is still so determined to learn dolphin talk. It is all she asks about now. I will try to teach her what I know. But it cannot be done with human language. I am thinking maybe, maybe it can be done with music.

Mr. Aradondo came to visit again today. He brought me a little cake.

I do not like the taste of sweets, but I know if someone gives a gift, it makes them sad if you do not want it. I remember so long ago when Sandy brought me the dead fish. I took the cake Mr. Aradondo made himself and I ate it, sharing it with the others. Mr. Aradondo is so quiet. I reach up and touch the blue marks on his arm. They make a picture of an anchor in the sea.

"Tattoo," Mr. Aradondo says. His teeth are not white like the teeth of Justin, but his smile is good. There is a piece of silver inside his mouth. Like the sun catching a lip of water. He does not pull away when I touch the tattoo.

"Are you born with this?" I ask.

Mr. Aradondo laughs. It is a laugh of yellow teeth. I see gray hairs inside his nose. "I had this done to me," he says.

I trace the outline with my fingers, shut my eyes, and listen. Mr. Aradondo's mind is as big as the ocean, as full of stories as the ocean is full of fish. I like the feel of Mr. Aradondo's mind.

It is not so tight as Doctor Beck, it is mostly open and full of light. I smile at him. He smiles back.

I am different from other humans. But they are different from one another. I sense their differences, the human who is Sandy, the human who is Doctor Beck, the human who is Mr. Aradondo. It is like the dolphins. The dolphins are different from one another. But the dolphins swim together, play together, live together. Most important to dolphins is to be together. I look at Justin. I have so much to learn about humans.

Human anger, human fear, these things get in the way for humans to feel good.

Anger is a sad thing to have. It makes the human alone. I look at Justin. I think about the clean animal smell of him. When I think of Justin, I think maybe it is not so important to return to my dolphin family, that I can stay with humans always. But Justin cannot be my mate. He is not wanting a dolphin girl. No human is wanting a dolphin girl.

Forty

Doctor Peach brings me music. He needs to show me only once. He plays for me. Then I play. My room is filled with sound. Doctor Peach brings musicians too with other instruments. I listen. I play my recorder with them. I no longer need to read the music like letters and words and sentences on a page. I speak it, I put the notes together into patterns.

Doctor Beck says my room is not a good place to make music. She asks people to come and make a quiet room in the house for me to play. The sound of my music upsets Shay. It upsets everyone who sleeps here. I don't want to upset Shay. But I am so full of music.

Justin takes me away from the classwork and the music and the time with the doctors. He plays games with me like basketball and soccer. We play in the walled yard behind our house and run through the bright sunlight all the way to Case Gymnasium, where the swimming pool is, and he makes me laugh and jump and run and stretch and kick and fly across the floor, chasing balls, chasing him. It is very good. But he does not change. He does not want to be touched. It is too hard to play with him the way the dolphins play, so full of joy, so full of movement, without the touching.

My music is not like Mozart. It is not like the music in the radio. But it is like the sound I know from the sea. I make a long song, all night, one song. Like the whale who is looking for a mate, I make a song that grows and changes and grows longer. The story becomes different stories, different patterns, making one big pattern. By the morning the song is not the same as I started in the night, but it is the same song. It has grown and changed. Justin brings his blanket and sits in the chair by the window and listens. Others come in to listen.

I forget that I am Mila. I forget everything. It is only the singing I hear. It is my singing.

Forty-one

I walk down the hall to see Shay. I watch her through the window in her door, sitting in a yellow chair, doing a finger play Doctor Beck taught us months ago. The plastic punching man is in Shay's room. Doctor Beck unlocks the door and lets me in.

Shay leans forward in her chair, facing Doctor Troy. Shay's hair is dark and all around her head. Her eyebrows are thick.

Doctor Troy sings about the dicky bird flying from a tree. He moves his hands to show the movement of the bird, first in front of him, then behind his back. Shay watches, her head tilted down, her eyes peering up through her lashes. She stumbles along, echoing the doctor. But even with the little dicky bird song, her voice does not sing. It shuffles through the sounds. It stumbles and trips over the notes.

Suddenly, as I watch Shay, I am angry at her, for what she is doing to the music.

She stares up at me from her chair. I can see, in her eyes, in the way she moves her head, she knows what I am thinking.

Doctor Troy takes Shay's hand and drags her to where I stand. "This is Mila," Doctor Troy says. "Do you remember Mila?"

Shay says *Mila*, but her voice is as flat as the windless sea.

"That's right, Shay," the doctor says. "Mila." The doctor makes a note in his book. *Shay says Mila*. Once they wrote, *Mila says Shay*. But that was so long ago.

Why have I come so far and not Shay?

Doctor Troy takes Shay by the hand and leads her back to her seat. He starts the same dicky bird song again. But Shay slides off her chair and sits on the floor, rocking.

It really doesn't matter about Shay and the locked door. Shay is locked inside herself.

I back out of the room. The inflated punching man brushes against my shoulder. Before I know what I am doing, I spin around, pull my hand back, and hit it.

The punching man swings backward, then snaps up to a standing position. The expression on its face never changes. It stands and takes the hit and still it smiles and waits for more.

Forty-two

I am filled with something that frightens me.

When I was with the dolphins, the rain lashed my skin, the waves choked my throat, I felt the sun blister me through a thirst of days. When I was with the dolphins, I did not always feel good in my body. But there was not this feeling.

When I first came, I was so close to Shay. Together we were different from the others. We were a pod of two.

But now Shay is left behind.

The music of Shay is no music at all, and yet it is Shay's music. If to be human means I can no longer hear the good rough music of Shay, then finally I am human.

I must ask Doctor Beck, I must ask Sandy, am I human enough?

Forty-three

I bring the recorder to Shay and help her to hold her hands over the smooth pale body of the instrument. I teach her to blow. Shay blows too hard. It hurts my ears. I feel the lick of anger, but I let it go, like the last sigh of a wave. Shay is happy to make the recorder shriek. If Shay is happy, let her play this way.

But I cannot listen. I go back to my room and leave my recorder with Shay.

Forty-four

Doctor Troy comes to my room early. He has a recorder. It is not my recorder. I know when I touch it. I know when I blow into it.

I give the recorder back to him. This is not mine.

Doctor Troy brings out another recorder. This one is broken in two pieces.

Shay has broken my recorder.

I sit on the floor of my room holding the broken pieces of my recorder, and I cry.

Forty-five

Sandy explains to me that Shay has stopped making progress. It's not entirely unexpected, Sandy says. The same thing has happened to every feral child ever studied. Every one, that is, except you.

Forty-six

Doctor Peach says, Please, Mila, I found a recorder very close to your old one. Please try it.

The feel is right, the sound is right.

But it doesn't matter. My music is fading. Inside me, everything is fading.

What I make on the new recorder is such a sad music. It has nothing to do with dolphin life.

Forty-seven

I must get back to the sea.

Forty-eight

I don't understand anymore what it was I tried to do with the music and dolphin talk for Doctor Beck. My mind cannot grasp the way the music flows unless I read it note for note on the page, following along slowly, simply, like the dicky bird song.

Shay is going away. The government funding for her to stay here has stopped. When I come into the room, she looks at me. She looks at me and I see her fear. She looks at me the way a solitary dolphin looks at a shark. Have I become one of the sharks?

But then her fear disappears and I see only an empty look in the eyes of Shay and I know she is already gone.

She is being moved tomorrow. To more locked doors. I think she knows. I think she knows enough now to know she has failed. She knows what it means to be locked in. She knows what it means to be alone. Before she came to Doctor Beck and Doctor Troy, she lived a life locked in and alone, but she did not know. Now she knows.

I go back to my room and get my old rubber boots. It has been many months since I wore them. I rub them together to make a dolphin sound. I stroke them with my hand. The good rubber feels like dolphin skin.

I bring the boots to Shay. Here, I say. A gift for you. Take them.

I make the dolphin sound for her with the boots. I put the boots on her feet and show her how to make the sound herself. Once that sound made Shay laugh. Now she lets me move her legs, but there is no laughter.

Shay is too tired to try anymore. She wants, but she doesn't know what she wants. It is too late for her to go back to what she was.

And what about me? What do I want? Is it too late for me to go back? I feel cold, and I put on a sweater. When I am hungry, I eat. I do not have to hunt for my food. I do not have to catch it or kill it. My food waits for me. I do not have to go for days with the thick-tongued thirst swelling my throat. When I am thirsty, I pour a glass of fresh water and I drink. I read books and I learn different stories. Mostly they are little stories, they fade like the sunset, like the picture the waves make on the sand, but they are important. I learn a little about my first home. Not the sea. About the people who were my first family. If I should go back anywhere, should I go back to them? They say they want me back, but I think they are not interested in the girl named Mila. I think they are not interested in the girl named Olivia. I think they are interested in the dolphin girl, only the dolphin girl. All my life with humans it will be this way. I will always be this dolphin girl. The humans will be curious the way the dolphin is curious about a piece of garbage floating on the sea. A thing to play with, a thing to drag and toss around, but in the end a thing to leave behind.

Forty-nine

Shay is gone.

I stood outside between Doctor Beck and Sandy and waved.

Shay stared straight ahead. She stared with dead fish eyes.

I sat on the stone curb for a long time after the car pulled away. The warm wind lifted a spiral of sand into the air. I don't know if it was the sand that made my tears come.

Shay was wearing my boots.

Fifty

During the night I dreamed a pod of dolphins beached itself outside my window. I ran out. I tried to get them back to sea, but as soon as I'd get one free, it would beach itself again.

I raced to the house for help. Please. We have to set them all free at once. They will not leave unless they all leave together.

Doctor Beck, Sandy, Justin, Mr. Aradondo, Doctor Troy. They all came. We managed to get the dolphins back in the water on the rising tide. The churned sand stung my legs like the biters that prowl the waving grasses on the margins of the sea. Everyone watched to see if I would go with the dolphins. The doctors, Mr. Aradondo, they thought I would go with the dolphins. The dolphins did not think I would

158

go with them. They knew I did not belong with them. I could not even make the call. I was a mouth speaker, not a nose speaker. They swam away from me. They swam away. I woke trying to remember the sound of their calls. I could not remember.

I go to Shay's room. It looks the same. Except the bed is empty. And there is an absence of Shay. Who will come into my room when I am gone and sing my story?

Fifty-one

I have no more appetite. I look at the food, but I cannot bring myself to eat. They will put the needle into my arm again. I cannot change what is happening. But their feeding tube cannot stop what is happening.

Fifty-two

Someone is always in my room. They keep me afloat. I do not know them all, though sometimes it is Doctor Beck or Justin. Sometimes it is Mr. Aradondo. Often it is Sandy. They talk to me. In English. In Spanish. Sometimes there is music. Sometimes there is not. I hear the murmurings of their thoughts. I feel their sadness as they watch me.

Justin unhooks my feeding tube. He and Doctor Beck help me to walk out of my room, down to the grass beach, to the Hump. The air is so warm. I hear the sounds. The cry of a gull. When I lay my head against the Hump, I hear the roll of waves. I hear the great sea lifting its tons, singing its long tale. I am in the wrong room in a very big house. If I keep walking down the long halls, will I find my way back to the sea?

I smile at Justin. He is close to his mother. He lets her arm come around his back. He lets her touch him. He leans into her. I say, You would make a very good dolphin, Justin Beck.

And you would make a very good human, Justin says.

But I am too weak. Too weak to make anything.

Fifty-three

I say, Doctor Beck, take me back to the island where the Coast Guard found me.

Doctor Beck looks at me the way she did when I asked for the doors to be unlocked. She explains again about the government money. She explains again about the government rules. She says, You are asking me to break the law. If I do what you ask, I will go to prison.

I look at her. I am already in prison.

Sandy says, We have to let her go.

What can they do to us that's any worse than what we've done to her? We have to let her go.

I am a face of bones.

Doctor Beck sees. What she sees is not a curiosity. It is not a laboratory experiment. Not a government project.

She sees me. The girl they call Mila.

She says, Maybe we could visit there, but you couldn't stay, Mila. I couldn't leave you there.

I need the roll of the sea, I need the gentle touch of the dolphin. I need home.

Fifty-four

The musicians come and play for me today. A private concert. Someone gives me a recorder. I cannot remember how to play. I cannot remember what the notes mean to the holes. I cannot make the notes on the sheet hold still. They swim up and down the staff, like dolphins.

Fifty-five

Sometimes I have trouble with the words. I try to catch them, but they slip away like little fish through a net. Doctor Beck says I can learn the words again, all the words and more words. They are all in the computer. They are all in my head. I only have to practice. To work. I do not want to work. Only to go home.

When I can go home?

Fifty-six

I am eating a little. I make a promise to Doctor Beck. I eat a little if she takes me to the sea.

Sandy is a good friend. She is here when I eat, when I sleep, when I wake. She says soft words. She is touching my hair. I love to close my eyes and feel her touching. She is my friend.

She says, Mila. We will take you to the sea.

Fifty-seven

I am on a boat. Doctor Beck is here. And Sandy. And Justin. Justin is smiling. The wind is in his hair. The air is soft and warm and gentle.

Home, I think. I am going home.

Fifty-eight

Doctor Beck and Sandy are happy.

There are dolphins swimming with the boat. I do not know these dolphins. I do not know this sea. This is not home.

Doctor Beck and Sandy think all dolphins are my family. But you cannot walk into any house and say, I am here, I am sick, take care of me. The people say, Who are you? You are a stranger.

I am a stranger to these dolphins.

They swim with the boat only because they like the ride.

Doctor Beck and Sandy do not understand. But Justin, he watches me. He hears what I cannot say. He understands.

Fifty-nine

I ask about Shay.

Doctor Beck says, Shay is happy. She lives in a big house with a man and a woman and other children. Doctor Troy went to see her, but she did not remember him.

Shay does not wait for me.

Are my dolphins waiting?

I'm so sorry, Mila, Doctor Beck says.

I am surprised. I am not sorry. I think of all the good things human. I think of Doctor Beck and Sandy and Justin. Justin sits with my hand in his hand. I cannot be sorry with Justin.

Justin says, What makes a whale beach itself? Are you beaching yourself, Mila?

I say, Justin. It is not difficult to understand. In the dolphin family, if one is lost, all are lost.

Justin is looking away.

Is it this way in the human family, I ask? I cannot know. No one is talking.

Doctor Beck comes to Justin. Her hand is on the back of Justin. Her lips are on the hair of Justin.

The dolphin, they live for today. But I am human. To be human is to live for tomorrow. Why does tomorrow matter? What is important is now.

Sixty

Is it that I can go with the dolphin and forget I am human?

It is difficult to think. I am tired.

Doctor Beck says, Mila, I know you hurt now. But it will not always hurt this way. Being human gets better. I promise.

Promise is a good thing. I know there is love and care for me, not just for the dolphin girl, but for me, Mila.

But it cannot get better. Even if Doctor Beck gives a promise. I have been coming back to the sea from the moment I left it.

Sixty-one

I know it. I know home. It is here. It is in me, a knowing of home. I do not understand. But in my heart there it is. I know. I know.

Sixty-two

My family comes. My family of dolphins comes. I am happy.

I look at them. I know their names.

They call me. My dolphin name. It
is my dolphin mother calling. It is
my dolphin aunt.

Give me to the water, I say.

Doctor Beck says, No. I can't do it.

Please, Doctor Beck. Give me to the
water.

Doctor Beck says, No. The dolphins may leave you to drown. They may turn on you.

They will not leave, they will not turn. I know them. They are my family.

Doctor Beck says, I'm afraid. What if you die in the water, Mila?

I will not die. Please, give me to the water, Doctor Beck.

Justin comes to me. He makes his arms around me. I close my eyes. It is so good. I am glad in the end to know the arms of Justin.

Justin says, I will give you to the water.

I watch the red sun set into a choppy sea. The wind brushes over my skin and tosses my hair like the long leaves of the palm. As I stand, looking west, all the world is water and I, with my two strong legs, with my strong heart and my deep lungs, I belong to it.

My dolphin family charges, mouths open, into a school of mullet. Seagulls glide overhead, eager for leavings. I stoop, stirring the water with my hands. I breathe in the air laced with seaweed and salt.

Waves whisper onto the beach, sucking at my heels and my toes. I gaze across the orange-tipped water, glad for each glimpse of my dolphin family surfacing.

A solitary brittle star brushes past my foot as it hunts for mussels in the twilight. I stand and walk slowly along the margin of the sea.

Around me the night creatures come to life, scurrying in the sand, creeping along blades of grass, nibbling sea oats.

I settle into my nest of leaves and make a sound high in my throat, a sound that forms a picture for my dolphin mother. I say good night to her, to my dolphin aunts, to my dolphin cousins.

Sweeping my hair back from my face, I breathe in the fresh night smells. It is the end of another dolphin day.

I sing my name to the first star. All that I am, all that I was, all that I ever will be, I put into my song.

My dolphin mother hears, and knows, and sings back.

Wrapping my arms around myself, all at once, unbidden, the past breaks over me. I'm awash in the memory of my fleeting human days; the play on the computer, the music of the recorder, the laughter of Shay. I remember the walks to the pool, and the talk of doctors, and the curiosity of strangers. I remember the sound of traffic, and the taste of sweet cake, and the smell of Sandy. I remember that last moment with the human boy, the beautiful human boy, and how the boat waited and waited so long for me I nearly returned.

This wanting has come before, and yet each time,

I am startled by the fierce and sudden hunger for things left behind.

But before long the wanting passes.

I cover myself with my long hair, turn toward the soft blowing of my dolphin family, and give myself to sleep.

About the Author

KAREN HESSE is the Newbery Medal-winning author of many acclaimed books for young readers, among them *Out of the Dust*, winner of the 1998 Newbery Medal and the Scott O'Dell Award; *Letters From Rifka*, winner of the Christopher Medal and the International Reading Association Award for Young Adult Fiction; *Phoenix Rising*, an ALA Best Book for Young Adults; and *The Music of Dolphins*, a *School Library Journal* and *Publishers Weekly* Best Book of the Year. Her most recent books include *Stowaway* and *The Cats in Krasinski Square*. She lives with her family in Brattleboro, Vermont.

Newbery Medalist Karen Hesse worl her magic in stories about life-sized problems and everyday heroes.

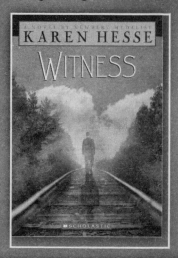